CREPE WORKERS

CROOKED BAY COZY MYSTERIES, BOOK 4

PATTI BENNING

SUMMER PRESCOTT BOOKS PUBLISHING

Copyright 2023 Summer Prescott Books

All Rights Reserved. No part of this publication nor any of the information herein may be quoted from, nor reproduced, in any form, including but not limited to: printing, scanning, photocopying, or any other printed, digital, or audio formats, without prior express written consent of the copyright holder.

**This book is a work of fiction. Any similarities to persons, living or dead, places of business, or situations past or present, is completely unintentional.

CHAPTER ONE

Theresa Tremblay spooned hollandaise sauce over the freshly made crêpe, then set the plate on the tray near the others. After wiping down the griddle, she carried the tray over to the waiting table.

"Two eggs Benedict crêpes and one strawberry and hazelnut spread crêpe," she said, placing the plates on the table in front of the people who had ordered them. "Enjoy! Let me know if you need anything else."

She smiled as she walked away, hearing her guests *ooh* and *ahh* over the food. Her restaurant, The Crooked Crêperie, was the only crêperie anywhere near the small town of Crooked Bay, and quite a few of the people she served had never had a real, French crêpe before.

Hearing and seeing her guests' happiness at trying a new dish for the first time brought her joy. It made all of the effort and energy she put into the restaurant worth it. She might not be making a huge difference in the world, but she was making people happy. This was something she could do to make the world a better place, even if it only happened one crêpe at a time.

Behind the counter, she set the tray down and waited for Josh, one of the two employees she had hired over a month ago, to finish taking an order so she could get started on it.

For the first couple of months after she opened the crêperie, she had been the only one working in it, and actually having employees now made all of the difference in the world. She no longer felt like she was struggling just to keep up.

"Look, boy, I told you what I wanted. I don't know why it's so hard for you to understand. I want a vegetarian crêpe, no cheese."

Theresa looked over at the man's sharp voice. He was a regular named Bill Mason, and he wasn't the most cheery person she had ever met. He came in a couple times a week, and always ordered his crêpes sans the sauce. He would get a banana hazelnut spread crêpe without the hazelnut spread, or chicken pesto crêpe without the pesto. He didn't seem to like anything that made the food too moist or gooey.

Josh, it seemed, took exception to that. "If you order a vegetarian crêpe without the cheese, you're literally just getting vegetables—"

"It's okay," Theresa interrupted. Josh was ... well, in a lot of ways he was an okay employee. He showed up on time, he did what she asked without complaint, and she trusted him to mop a floor or cut vegetables. But when it came to actually interacting with the customers, she'd had to intercede a few times. He could get snippy, especially if there was a disagreement or misunderstanding between him and the customer. She had talked to him about it, but it hadn't made any difference. Now, she stepped forward, smiling at Bill apologetically. "He knows what he wants, Josh. He's been here before."

"Whatever," Josh grumbled, typing the order in. Theresa returned to the griddle and ladled some fresh batter onto it. Josh told Bill the total, took his money, and counted out the change. As soon as the receipt was printed, Bill moved over to watch her prepare the food.

As he walked away, Josh grumbled, "Ugly old fart."

Bill froze. Theresa turned slowly to look at her

employee, a prickly mix of anger and embarrassment rising even as Bill stalked back over to the register.

"What did you say?"

Josh smirked. "Nothing."

"My hair might be grey, but I'm not *that* old. I can still hear. Is this the way you treat your customers?"

"Josh, can you go into the kitchen?" Theresa asked, her voice tight. "Please."

For a second, she thought her employee was going to argue, but then he heaved a deep sigh and slouched away. Theresa turned her attention back to Bill.

"I'm so sorry," she said, already tapping the code to open the cash register. She counted cash and coins out and handed it over to him. "You'll get your crêpe for free today, and next time you come in, you'll get another one on the house. Josh was completely out of line. I can't apologize enough."

Bill took the money, frowning. "I don't know if I'll be coming back."

She hesitated, then lowered her voice. "It won't happen again. I promise. I hope you keep coming here. I value my regulars a lot."

He gave a brief nod and returned to the plastic divider in front of the griddle to wait for his food. She discarded the overcooked crêpe on top of it and started fresh, making sure the crêpe was perfect before she slipped it into a to-go box and handed it over. He gave a grunt of thanks and left. As soon as the door shut behind him, Theresa leaned against her stool and let out a long sigh.

She was going to have to fire Josh. She had thought, or hoped, his attitude was something they could work on, but he had gone too far. She couldn't have her employees insulting her customers to their faces.

The trio she had served a few minutes ago were still eating their crêpes but were eyeing her, having overheard a good portion of the confrontation. She gave them a tight smile, wiped down her griddle, then went into the kitchen to ask Josh to spend the rest of the afternoon cleaning and prepping.

She would wait until close to let him go. She felt bad enough about deciding to fire him as it was—she didn't want to take away anything from his last paycheck. He needed the money to pay his rent and bills. She knew he didn't have a car at the moment, and the crêperie was walking distance from the apartment he shared with his roommate. In a lot of ways, it was the perfect job for him.

She hated knowing her decision meant he might not be able to make ends meet this month, and she spent the rest of her shift swallowing against the sourness in her throat, dreading each tick of the second hand as the clock on the wall ticked closer to three.

She locked the doors as soon as the last customer walked out that afternoon and began cleaning up the bits of trash that had spread throughout the dining area during the day. She knew she was procrastinating, but she wanted to put it off as long as she could. She had never fired someone before and didn't know how to begin.

When Josh came out of the kitchen and walked over to the computer by the register to clock out, she put her broom down. "Josh? Can I talk to you for a second?"

He frowned. "My friends are going to pick me up. We've got plans this afternoon. It won't take long, will it?"

She shook her head. Unconcerned, he turned to the computer and punched in his code. Biting her lip, she tried to plan out what she was going to say, how to say it. Her heart was beating too fast. Why was this so hard?

Just as he finished clocking out, someone rapped on the glass of the front door. Theresa turned and saw two people about Josh's age standing outside; one was a pretty young woman with dark brown, almost black hair pulled back into a short ponytail with fuchsia streaks coloring it, and the other was a young man with light brown hair wearing a band T-shirt. They both waved at Josh, and Josh went over to unlock the door and let them in. Normally, Theresa wouldn't care, but now she cleared her throat.

"Josh, I still need to talk to you."

He looked over at her impatiently. "Look, I gotta go. I'm working tomorrow, so we can talk then, yeah?"

She wasn't scheduled to work tomorrow herself, but even if she was, she didn't want to put this off any longer. "Josh, will you please come into the kitchen with me? I want to talk to you privately."

His friend — she recognized him as his roommate, Adrian, from the times he had stopped in for discounted crêpes while Josh was working — let out a quiet, "Ooh, you're in trouble."

Josh sighed. "Sorry, guys, it'll just take a sec." He fist-bumped Adrian and paused to give the girl a quick kiss. "I'll be quick, Tabitha."

"We'll wait," she promised with a smile.

Josh followed Theresa into the kitchen, frowning at her as he slumped through the door. "What's this about?"

Theresa took a deep breath. "I'm sorry, Josh, but I'm going to have to let you go."

"What?" He stared at her. "Are you firing me?"

"I've had to address multiple issues with your customer service, and today, with Bill, was the last straw. I'm sorry, Josh. I hope—"

"I can't believe this!" His voice rose into a shout as he cut her off. "You're just firing me, just like that? What am I supposed to do? I need this job. I need the money. Am I even getting paid for today?"

"Of course. I'll have your check ready for you in a few—"

"I can't believe this! This is bull." He turned, kicked at a cupboard, and slammed his way through the door to the dining area. She followed him.

"Josh! Will you talk to me? I'm not done."

"Let's go," he snapped. Both his friends looked confused and, in Tabitha's case, concerned. "We're getting out of here."

He ignored their questions as he strode through the door, toward the car that was parked along the curb. Adrian took a key fob out of his pocket and pressed a button, the car chirped as it unlocked. Theresa pushed through the restaurant's door behind them, still trying to get Josh's attention.

"Josh! Would you just wait one second? You need to—"

Josh paused, then turned around slowly. His eyes

darted to the side, and she saw a couple of pedestrians who had paused to take in the scene. Someone else was walking a dog down the sidewalk. The only warning she had was the smirk that came across his face before he raised his voice loud enough to carry.

"I've had enough! I'm not going to work somewhere that won't even let me wash my hands after touching raw chicken, and I'm not going to just sit back while your customers hurl abuse at me. I quit!"

"Josh?" Tabitha asked. "What's—"

He shook his head and gestured for her to get in the car. She did as Adrian slipped into the driver's seat, giving his friend a puzzled look. Josh paused, looking back at Theresa as the onlookers started to mutter.

"I hope you go out of business," he said, his voice low and filled with venom. "You deserve it."

Then he got into the car, slamming the passenger side door, and Adrian pulled away with a squeal of tires on the pavement.

CHAPTER TWO

The next day was supposed to be Theresa's day off. She had one day off scheduled each week, and she treasured them after spending so long working each and every day, but with Josh gone, she had to go in. It was pouring rain, and the dreary weather matched her mood perfectly.

Wynne was surprised to find Theresa instead of Josh when she arrived.

"I must've had the schedule wrong," the younger woman said with a tight laugh as she put her purse on the counter. "Not that I'm complaining. Today should be fun."

"No, you didn't have the schedule wrong," Theresa said. "Josh is no longer working here."

Wynne's eyebrows rose. "What happened?"

Theresa hesitated, but she didn't see a reason to keep the truth from her only other employee. "He was extremely rude to a customer yesterday, and it was the last in a long line of issues. I decided to let him go. And we owe Bill Mason a free crêpe, don't let me forget."

To her surprise, Wynne blew a strand of hair out of her face and grinned. "I can't say I'm sad about that. Or surprised."

"Did you not like working with him?" Theresa asked as she took a cutting board out. Food prep was the most time-consuming part of the opening routine. The other woman leaned against the counter.

"He was just... I don't know how to explain it, really. There was an undertone to all of our interactions that made me uncomfortable. Like the first thing he saw when he looked at me was a pretty woman, not a person or a coworker." She gave Theresa a look out of the corner of her eye. "You understand what I mean, right? I think it's something most women have experienced."

Theresa nodded slowly, feeling a sinking sensation in her gut. "I'm sorry, Wynne. I didn't realize."

The other woman shrugged. "I would've said something if he got worse about it. I'm just glad I don't have to now."

"You should've come to me right away," Theresa said. She hoped she didn't sound accusing, because that wasn't how she meant it. "I don't want any of my employees to be uncomfortable. Or my guests, for that matter. I hope you *will* come to me in the future if you're having troubles with anyone—whether it's the next person we hire, or one of our customers." She wrinkled her nose slightly. "Assuming anyone wants to work for us now."

Wynne raised an eyebrow. "What do you mean?"

Theresa sighed. "Let's just say, firing him didn't exactly go well. He stomped out of the restaurant before I was done talking, and once we were outside, he made a scene. There were a few people on the sidewalk, and he went off about how I was asking him to follow unsafe practices in the kitchen and expected him to just sit back and let customers be rude to him. He made it sound like he was quitting because I was a terrible boss, not the other way around."

"I can't believe him," Wynne scoffed. "Good riddance. I know it will mean more work for both of us until you hire someone new, but it's worth it."

It was pleasant, working with Wynne that day. Unlike Josh, Wynne always had her best foot forward with the guests. If anything, she was even better at talking and laughing with them than Theresa was. Despite the fact that she was supposed to have been off today, the hours passed by quickly.

Toward the end of the day, she opened the coat cabinet in the back of the kitchen to check for a spare phone charger, since the one she had with her wasn't working, when she saw Josh's hoodie hanging up and his hat sitting on the top shelf. He had left yesterday before she could remind him to grab his things, and now she sighed and reached for her phone. She didn't want to talk to him again, but she also didn't want to have to hold his items indefinitely until he remembered to come get them.

She called him and he answered with a short, "What?"

"Hi, Josh," she said, keeping her voice civil. "I didn't get a chance to remind you yesterday, but you still have a few of your things here. Can you stop by soon and get them?"

"I guess. What about my check?"

They weren't due to be paid until early next week, but she wanted to be done with this, so she sighed and said, "I'll have your check ready too. When will you be able to stop by?"

He heaved a sigh as if she was asking him for a

huge favor. "I'll see if Tabitha can give me a ride now, I guess. I'm not walking in this rain."

He hung up before she could say anything else. Before she forgot, she calculated his hours, wrote out a check, and put it in the cabinet on the shelf next to his hat. Then, she returned to the front where Wynne was finishing up a crêpe for one of the regulars. While her employee cleaned off the griddle, Theresa took a spot by the register and gazed out the window at the rain steadily dribbling down.

"Josh is going to stop by soon," she told Wynne quietly. "I'm hoping he'll be here before close. He's going to grab his things and his check."

Wynne wrinkled her nose. "I bet he's going to cause a scene."

Theresa grimaced. She hadn't thought of that—maybe she should have asked him to come after close. "Why don't you get going a few minutes early? You shouldn't have to deal with him."

Wynne hesitated. "I'd feel bad leaving you on your own."

Theresa waved her off. "I'm the one who got us into this mess by hiring him in the first place. I'll deal with it."

The other woman hesitated a moment longer. "Are you sure?"

Theresa nodded. "It's fine. I'll cover the last few minutes here myself. You go ahead and go."

She knew she had done the right thing when she saw the relief in the other woman's face. Wynne clocked out, stepped into the back to grab her purse, then waved a quick goodbye before leaving, going out through the employee entrance in the back. Theresa spent the next few minutes waiting by the register, but no one else came in. When her last guests left, she locked the front door and started cleaning. She kept glancing out the front, wondering if Josh would come in through there or through the back. He still had his key, and she would need to remember to get it back from him. She sighed. This whole mess was stressful. Hopefully, she had better luck with his replacement. Wynne was great, but she didn't want a repeat of Josh.

She was about to go and check the kitchen in case he had come in through the employee entrance when she heard a loud bang from the back of the building. For a second, she wondered if it was a car backfiring, but her gut told her otherwise. She'd grown up here in Michigan, had been around rural areas during deer season. She knew what a gunshot sounded like.

Dropping her rag, she hurried into the kitchen and then through the back door. As she pushed the door open, she heard the sound of tires squealing against the pavement, but she wasn't fast enough to see the vehicle before it peeled away.

It didn't matter anyway. She couldn't look away from the person lying on the wet pavement of the small rear parking lot. Rain pattered down, already diluting the blood spreading beneath the too-still form.

CHAPTER THREE

"Josh!"

She ran forward, her feet splashing through the puddles in the parking lot behind the building. As she fell to her knees, she ignored the puddle that dampened the legs of her jeans and pressed a hand to the gunshot wound on his chest, trying to stop it, to seal it somehow.

He was still warm, but his body was too still, and his eyes were open and unblinking even as drops of rain fell on his face.

"Josh, come on, it's going to be okay." She shook him with her other hand, but he didn't respond.

He wasn't bleeding as much as she thought someone would when they had just been shot—and she realized that must mean his heart had stopped beating.

This couldn't be real. Not even five minutes ago, she had been dreading seeing him again, but there was no world in which she wouldn't rather put up with him yelling at her than *this*.

She might not have been on good terms with him, but she didn't want him to be *dead*.

"Hey!" She looked up and saw that an elderly woman had come out of the rear entrance to one of the neighboring buildings. "Who is that?"

She stood up, the knees of her pants wet from the rain. "You need to call the police, he's been shot—"

"What are you doing to that man? Get away from him."

The woman had seen Josh's still form. Theresa backed away, her hands spread wide. "I didn't do anything. We need an ambulance—"

"I'm calling 911."

Since that was what she wanted the woman to do, she didn't argue, but as she listened to the woman give her version of events to the dispatcher, a new kind of dread enveloped her.

This wasn't her fault. It *wasn't*.

But would the police believe her?

A crowd had gathered by the time the ambulance

and the police cruisers arrived. It was a small crowd, because the rain was still coming down and the parking lot behind the buildings along Main Street didn't get much traffic, but it still felt like too much to Theresa. She stood with her back pressed against the crêperie's wall as they muttered, their eyes sharp and wary as they looked from Josh's body to her.

The police moved the crowd back as the paramedics approached. They kneeled beside Josh and felt for a pulse. It didn't take long for them to shake their heads. One of the officers went over and exchanged a few words with them. He raised a radio to his mouth and with a crackle of static, called a code into the sheriff's department.

While the paramedics gathered their tools and backed away, the officer approached the woman who had called 911. Theresa watched as they spoke, wondering what the other woman was saying about what had happened. She saw the woman gesture at her, and the officer turned to look at her, a frown on his face. She recognized him—he was Officer Fenwick, a young man just a little older than Josh had been. He had been the one who responded back when someone had vandalized the crêperie. At the time, he had been friendly, if not exactly helpful. Now, the friendly expression was gone, and he looked at her like she was some dangerous thing that might become a threat again at any moment.

"Ms. Tremblay?" he asked as he approached her. He adjusted his cap, which was keeping the worst of the rain off his face.

"What do you need from me?" She knew they would need something. Josh had been her employee, after all, and she had been the one who found him. She just hoped the need for her involvement stopped there.

"Can you tell me what happened here? Do you know this man?"

"His name is Josh Clarke," she said, her voice wavering only slightly. "He's my employee—or, he was. I fired him yesterday. He came here today to pick up some personal items he left behind. His girlfriend was supposed to give him a ride here." She thought about Tabitha. Where was she? She was supposed to have given him a ride, but she was nowhere to be seen. Was she okay? Was she involved, somehow? "I heard a gun go off, and when I came out to investigate, I found him like this."

"I see." The suspicion on his face hadn't faded. "I'm afraid I'm going to have to ask you to—"

"My security cameras!" she blurted out, her eyes widening as the thought occurred to her. She looked up and there, nestled above the rear door to the crêperie, was a little white camera. She had installed one there and one at the front door when she first bought the building and had been having the issues with vandalism. She didn't remember the last time she had checked them, but there it was, its little red light glowing. "It might have seen something."

Officer Fenwick followed her gaze. "We'll need access to the footage," he said. "Sit tight for a few more minutes. I've called for backup. Once they arrive, we will get the footage from the cameras. And then, you're going to need to come into the station with us."

She nodded, ignoring the tight coil of nerves in her chest. She knew she was innocent. And she was sure the cameras would prove it. But until they let her go, a part of her was going to dread whatever came next.

By the time backup arrived and she had given Officer Fenwick the login information for the camera footage, which was stored on the cloud, over an hour had passed. She rode in the back seat of Officer Fenwick's car, not handcuffed but trapped nonetheless. The police station was brightly lit and warm, and it was a relief to be out of the rain, if nothing else.

Officer Fenwick led her to an interrogation room

and left her alone in there with a cup of water—he had offered her coffee but she had declined, knowing the caffeine would only make her nerves worse—and a stale muffin. She picked at the food and sipped the water while she waited. The clock on the wall told her another forty-five minutes had passed before Officer Fenwick returned. As he sat in the chair across the table from her, she saw that some of the wariness had left his face.

"We reviewed the footage, and unfortunately, it does not show the attack," he told her, cutting right to the chase.

She deflated. "It didn't see anything?"

"It caught the sound of the gun discharging, but the rain muffled everything else. The event itself happened out of frame. It did, however, verify that you did not leave your building until after the gun went off. You're free to go, Ms. Tremblay, after we ask you just a few more questions. We need to know everything you remember about Josh over the past few days. If he knew who killed him, he might have said something to you or to a coworker that can help us figure out this mess."

Relief washed through her, though it was tinged with guilt and sadness. She was going to walk free—but Josh wouldn't ever walk anywhere again.

Taking a deep breath, she started talking, doing her best to remember every single thing Josh had said over the past few days. She didn't know if any of it was important, but even if she hadn't picked up a gun and shot him herself, it was her fault Josh had been out there that afternoon. She owed it to him to do everything in her power to make sure his killer was caught.

CHAPTER FOUR

Theresa made the decision to close the crêperie down temporarily out of respect for her employee. Granted, Josh hadn't been an employee at the time of his death, but that was a technicality. Everything had happened so fast, and she wished she could go back in time and undo it all. She had been mad at Josh, and disappointed, yes, but she hadn't wanted him *dead*.

The whole thing made her feel sick and sad, and she spent that Friday morning halfheartedly tidying her apartment, wishing there was something more worthwhile she could do. Somewhere out there, Josh's family was grieving for him. And here she was, puttering around her home and wiping the counters. It didn't feel right.

When her phone rang, she practically lunged for

it, glad for the distraction. She wasn't surprised to see Jace's name on the caller ID. She had told her son all about what had happened the night before—she had kept enough from him over these past few months and had promised there would be no more secrets—and it was just like him to want to check up on her.

"I'm surviving," she said when he asked her how she was doing. "I don't think I'll reopen the crêperie until next week. I'll be losing money, but it wouldn't feel right. I have no idea how I'm going to occupy myself for that long, but I'll figure something out."

"Has there been any progress on the case?" Jace asked, his voice hopeful.

"Not as far as I know. I've been checking online, but there aren't any updates yet. I feel so *guilty,* Jace. I know it's not my fault, but I was the one who asked him to be there. How did this turn into such a mess?"

"I know it's hard, but you shouldn't blame yourself." He sighed. "I'm sorry you have to deal with all of this, Mom. I can try to take some time off—"

"No." She felt a little bad for interrupting him, but pressed on anyway. "You just started that job, and it's an amazing opportunity for you. You stay right where you are. I know you're worried about me, and I understand because I'd be worried about you if our situations were reversed, but you have to believe me when I say I'll be all right. I've got Clare here if I need company, so I'm not completely alone."

He relented but told her he would try to come and visit her soon anyway. Just talking to him warmed her heart, and she told him as much. While she missed him horribly now that he lived in Michigan's Upper Peninsula, and far away from her own home in the lower part of the state, knowing he was doing well made happiness and pride swell in her heart. It wasn't enough to chase the guilt over Josh away, but it helped.

When a knock sounded at her apartment door, she said, "Speaking of not being alone, I think that's Clare now. I'd better get going, sweetie. I'll let you know if there are any updates later today."

"All right. Tell Clare I say hi."

She promised she would, then ended the call and walked over to the door, pausing to look out the peephole. Sure enough, her cousin was waiting on the other side. She unlocked the door, and Clare came in, giving her a brief, tight hug before slipping off her shoes.

"I don't see you for a few days, and you find trouble again?" The other woman shook her head. "I thought *I* was supposed to be the troublemaker in this family."

Theresa huffed a laugh and walked into the living room, the other woman following her. "Maybe it's just this town. It makes trouble magnets out of all of us. Can I get you anything? Coffee, tea?"

"I'm fine for now," Clare said, flopping down onto the couch. She looked out the patio window and at the bay beyond. It was a gray day today, but not raining anymore at least. "How are you doing, really? I know we talked last night, but I also know things tend to look different in the light of day. Sometimes better, sometimes worse, so which is it?"

Theresa sighed. "I'll tell you what I told Jace: I'm holding on. I feel horrible and guilty about what happened, but what can I do? I feel so helpless, and I hate it. I've been miserable all morning, but it's not fixing anything. This isn't something that *can* be fixed."

"I don't have any good answers for you," Clare said. "Death is hard, especially when it happens to someone young."

Theresa sank into the armchair across from her cousin. "Do you want to know a secret? There is a part of me, and not a small part, that is worried about my reputation, of all things. Not Josh's death or his killer walking free, but what's going to happen to the crêperie after all of this." She sighed. "That makes me a terrible person, doesn't it?"

"Of course not." Clare looked at her, aghast. "It just makes you human. I don't see how anyone could possibly blame the crêperie for what happened, though."

Theresa wrinkled her nose. "The police were a hair away from arresting me last night. It wouldn't surprise me if word got out that his death had something to do with the Crooked Crêperie. I fired him the day before he died, and he made a scene outside the restaurant. The next day, he's murdered in the parking lot behind it? The town's not going to forget this, Clare."

"Once the police catch his killer, they'll forget all about his link to the crêperie."

"But how long will that take? My security cameras didn't catch anything. I don't think anyone saw anything. It was raining hard, so any physical evidence would have washed away. The police are trying their hardest, but without any evidence, what can they do?" She shook her head. "This isn't helping. Can we change the subject?"

"Of course," her cousin said. "What do you want to talk about?"

Theresa forced a small smile to her face. "How's work going?"

"It's going pretty well, actually. I started doing online readings, finally. It took me a while to get it figured out, but I've got a good system for it now. I don't like doing them as much as I like the in-person readings, but it lets me expand my client base a *lot*."

Clare made her living as a psychic ... sort of. She was open to Theresa that she didn't believe in that sort of thing, but she put on airs for her clients and believed she was helping them by letting them bounce their own thoughts and feelings off her. It was, she liked to put it, cheap therapy with an unlicensed therapist.

"That's good, Clare. I'm happy for you. How about that mystery man? Are you still seeing him? Am I ever going to meet him?"

Clare's eyes lit up. "Actually, I was just talking with him about that yesterday, before I got your call. He's been bothering me about meeting my family and friends too, so I finally agreed to give in and make you both happy. Do you want to have dinner with the two of us next week? Wednesday would work well for us, but we could probably do a different day if it doesn't work for you."

"I would love to have dinner with the two of you

next Wednesday," Theresa said. "Just let me know when and where."

Clare nodded. "I will. Is there anyone you want to bring?" There was a glint in her eye, and Theresa hesitated. For a second, she thought of Liam, the soft-spoken bookstore owner she had started up a tenuous friendship with. There was something between them, or the promise of something that could be if they both wanted it, but…

"No," she said, forcing a small laugh. "Just me, like always."

Maybe in another lifetime, she would have pursued that promise of *something* between her and Liam. But she didn't think there was room for romance in her life, not anymore.

Not again.

CHAPTER FIVE

After so long spent working at the crêperie every day, suddenly not going in for multiple days in a row left Theresa at loose ends. She went on walks, tried to follow Josh's case though there wasn't much to follow, and met Clare for lunch on Friday. By the time Saturday came around, she had to admit that she was … bored. It was a terrible admission, even in the privacy of her own mind, but she couldn't deny that it was the truth.

She was standing in front of her open fridge, trying to decide whether she had enough food to make herself something for lunch or if she wanted to go to the grocery store when she realized she had a whole fridge full of fresh ingredients that were just going to spoil by the time she opened the crêperie again. The frozen items would be okay, of course, but the fresh produce and meat would not last all the way until next week.

She didn't have much to make at the apartment, and rescuing food from the crêperie made a lot more sense than going to the grocery store, so she got ready to go out, locked up, and headed into town. The sun was shining, and the sidewalks were full of pedestrians taking advantage of the early summer weather. It felt good to be out of the apartment, and she decided to stop by the beach before she went home, even if just for a few minutes. She loved living on the lake, but she hadn't taken advantage of it much yet. She could chalk it up to being busy or that it was still early in the season, but she knew the real reason was she just wasn't used to going on outings like that on her own. For most of her life, up until Nick passed away, activities like going to the beach or going on hikes had been a family affair. Now, with her husband buried and her son living hours away, it was just her.

She let herself into the crêperie through the front, not wanting to park behind the building so soon after finding Josh's body there. She would have to force herself to do it eventually, but she knew that if she went back there right now, all she would be able to think of was Josh lying far too still in the rain as the last of the life seeped from him.

She locked the crêperie's door behind her, turned the radio on, and propped the door to the kitchen open so she could listen to music while she went through the refrigerator. She rescued a couple of chicken breasts, putting them in a paper bag with some bagged ice to keep them cool, and grabbed some peppers, a few tomatoes, and a bunch of lettuce. It looked like the makings of a decent salad, so she snagged part of a block of cheese as well.

She was looking over the avocados, trying to find the ones that were on the verge of being overripe, when she heard the sharp sound of someone knocking on the glass of the front door. She carefully set the avocados down, then walked out into the dining area. Someone was standing in front of the crêperie's door, their hands cupped to look through the glass. Theresa walked over to the radio and turned the music down, then approached the door. Once she got close enough to see the other person clearly, she recognized Josh's girlfriend, Tabitha. Her face was puffy, and her eyes were red, and she gave Theresa a look of such despair that Theresa unlocked the door and pulled it open without a second thought.

"Are you all right?" she asked, stepping back as

the younger woman came into the restaurant. "Do you need help?"

Tabitha sniffed and dragged a sleeve across her eyes. "Why?" she asked, her voice thick from crying. "What did I ever do to *you*?"

The accusation in her voice took Theresa aback. "What do you mean?"

"You told them *I* did it." Her voice broke. She crossed her arms, clinging tightly to the ends of her sleeves. "You told the police I killed Josh."

Her mind raced as she tried to figure out why Tabitha was accusing her of something so horrible. She came up blank. She didn't have the faintest idea who had killed Josh, and she certainly hadn't accused the woman standing in front of her of it.

"I'm sorry, but I don't know what you're talking about. I haven't accused anyone of—"

"They told me it was you!" Tabitha let out a sharp breath and breathed in slowly, as if calming herself. "The police brought me in for questioning, and they told me Josh's employer had said *I* gave him a ride to the crêperie that afternoon. They thought *I* was the one who brought him here —that I had something to do with him getting *shot* and *dying*. I don't understand why you would tell them something like that. Is this some sort of messed up revenge for how he acted when you fired him?"

So that was it? Theresa frowned. "Josh told me you were going to give him a ride," she explained. "I asked him to come by and get the items he had left here. He said he would be over shortly, and he was going to ask you to give him a ride since it was raining. I just told the police what he told me. I'm so sorry that you had to go through that."

"I wasn't even in town," Tabitha said, her voice cracking again. "Do you have any idea what it was like to be told my boyfriend was *dead* and then realize I was a suspect in the next moment? I had no idea what was going on."

"I'm sorry," Theresa said. Her voice sounded too small. She didn't know what to say, or how to help. "He didn't deserve what happened to him, and neither did you. I wish I knew who to blame, but I don't."

Tabitha sniffed and mumbled, "Do you have any tissues?"

Theresa nodded. She told the younger woman to take a seat, then went to get the tissues out of the back. She handed the box over and gingerly sat down across from the other woman. She was full of questions. If Tabitha hadn't given Josh a ride, then had Adrian done it? Or had Josh ended up walking, or calling a ride from one of those rideshare apps, or getting a ride from a stranger? Did he have other friends in the area who might have dropped him off?

She held her tongue, though—as much as she wanted to know more about what had happened, she could tell Tabitha wasn't in any place to talk about it. Instead, she waited in silence until the younger woman had dabbed her tears away and could talk without crying.

"Thank you for explaining things to me," she said at last, her voice still quiet. All of the anger had left her, and all that was left was a quiet sort of sadness. "I'm sorry for dumping all of that on you. I just... I haven't been able to think straight these past few days."

"It's okay," Theresa said, her voice gentle. "I understand. Take as much time as you need."

The other woman nodded and grabbed another tissue. Before she could blow her nose again, someone else knocked on the crêperie's door, and then pushed it open. Theresa turned, ready to tell whoever was coming in to leave because they were closed, but then spotted Liam. His brows were drawn close in concern as he glanced between her and Tabitha.

"I saw your car out front and thought I'd stop by, but if this isn't a good time, I can go."

Theresa did want to see him, but she didn't want to push Tabitha out. She was about to tell him to come back in a few minutes, but Tabitha stood before she could say anything. "I'd better get going. I think I'm going to go home and hide in my bed for a while." She gave a weak smile. "Thanks for talking to me."

"Of course," Theresa said, standing up as well. "Do you want anything before you go? We have a coffee machine, or I could make you a crêpe…"

The other woman shook her head. "I haven't had much of an appetite since … everything. I'm just going to go."

Theresa trailed behind her until they reached the door, then watched as Tabitha started walking away, her hands in her pockets and her head drooping. She was the picture of misery, and Theresa's heart went out to her. She knew how it felt to lose a loved one.

"Was she someone you know?" Liam asked once Tabitha was out of earshot.

Theresa shook her head, then shrugged. "She's Josh's girlfriend. She was upset about a misunderstanding from when the police questioned her. I feel bad for her. I hope she can find some peace."

Liam turned to her, his dark eyes worried. "How about you? How are you doing?"

She grimaced. It was a complicated answer, but … it wasn't as if she had anything pressing to do.

"Do you want to help me sort through some produce? We can talk while we work."

CHAPTER SIX

Liam helped her load her car with her rescued groceries while she told him about Tabitha's visit and her own feelings of being stuck and helpless with the crêperie closed and no updates on Josh's case. Her stomach growled as she put the gallon of milk in the back seat, and she sighed, realizing that she still had to go home and actually cook her meal. She hadn't had lunch yet, and she was hungry.

She shut her car door, spent a moment considering how long the bags of ice she had packed would keep her perishables cold, then glanced at Liam. "Do you want to grab lunch at Club King with me?"

He checked his watch. She knew he shut his bookstore for an hour at lunch—that hour seemed to migrate from day to day, and she wondered just how crazy that drove his customers—and she wasn't sure how long he had been gone already. He only thought about it for a moment before agreeing.

"I could do with a sandwich. Do you want to walk?"

She nodded. It was just down and across the street from the crêperie. The day was nice, and there was no reason not to get a little bit of exercise. This outing would have to replace her trip to the beach, since she didn't want her food to spoil, but it would be nice to spend time with someone who was … well, by now she thought she could consider him a friend.

They walked down to Club King together and joined the line at the counter. It seemed busier than usual, and she wondered if her usual customers from the crêperie had gone here for lunch instead. She glanced around, and spotted at least one regular up by the register—Bill Mason, the same man who had led to her firing Josh.

She watched Dora, the deli's owner, hand him a sandwich. He walked over to an empty table, where he opened the to-go bag and checked his order. His lips thinned, and he shoved the sandwich back into the bag and walked up to the counter.

"Excuse me," he said, his tone sharp. When Dora looked over with raised eyebrows, he continued, "I asked for no mayo on the sandwich, and you gave me mayo. You need to fix this. I'm not going to eat it like this."

Dora, the sandwich shop's owner, sighed, but kept an apologetic smile on her face. "I'm sorry about that, Mr. Mason. I'll make you a new one real quick. You can keep or toss the old one."

He still looked unhappy but retreated to the end of the counter to wait. Dora switched with an employee to make his sandwich herself, and he left without thanking her. Theresa watched him go, her lips pressed together.

"I understand his frustration if his order wasn't right, but he could be a bit more polite about it," she muttered to Liam as they moved forward in the line.

"I've had him in at the bookstore, and he's always a little ornery." He shrugged. "It might be different if I had employees who he was treating poorly, but I don't mind so much when it's just me."

Liam not only kept odd hours, but he ran the bookstore by himself. It was closed on Mondays, so he had one day a week off, but having experienced running the crêperie on her own for so long, she didn't see how he could manage working six days a week year-round at the bookstore for years on end without going insane.

Of course, it wasn't as if he had to juggle cooking, food preparation, and cleaning on top of manning the register. She mused the differences between their two businesses as the line shortened. Finally, they were able to put their own orders in. Theresa was in the mood for something warm, so she got a panini while Liam ordered the restaurant's namesake and got a club sandwich. Since they were going to eat in, they took their number and went over to a table by the window to wait.

"When do you plan on reopening?" he asked once they were seated.

"Wednesday next week," Theresa told him. "There's a food delivery scheduled for that morning, and I don't want more of our fresh food to go to waste. Losing the sales from this week will be hard enough, but it wouldn't have felt right to keep serving crêpes like nothing happened."

"It must be hard, losing an employee like that."

She frowned, fiddling with the plastic number Dora had handed them. "That's the thing, though. He wasn't an employee. I had fired him just the day before. He was only there to pick up some personal belongings that afternoon."

"Ah, I hadn't heard that. I'm not sure if that makes it easier or more difficult."

She gave him a grim smile. "I'm not sure either. Out of curiosity, what *have* you heard about what happened?"

He shrugged. "Different stories. Most people don't really seem to know what happened other than that a man was shot in town. I heard one person say you got into a fight with your employee and shot him yourself, but that was just an absurd rumor."

"It's not as bad as I'd feared at least. I fired him the day before, like I said, but he didn't take it well. He made a big scene outside the crêperie and made it sound like he was quitting because of how terrible the crêperie was. A few people overheard him, but it sounds like they haven't spread too many rumors about it. I supposed I have that to be grateful for."

"Keep in mind, my bookstore isn't exactly a hotspot for town gossip. What I know might not be a good measure for what the general sentiment around town is."

She knew he was right, even though it wasn't comforting. She hated worrying about her reputation when a man was dead, but at the same time, the crêperie was her livelihood. She had put everything into it. How could she *not* be worried about it?

"Lunch for two!" Theresa looked around at the cheery voice and spotted Dora approaching, carrying their food on a platter. She smiled at the woman, who was somewhere between an acquaintance and a friend. Dora glanced at Liam and then winked at her as she set the food down. Theresa forced herself to not roll her eyes—what was with everyone thinking she and Liam were more than just friends?

"I'm glad to see you out and about," Dora said, leaning against the table. One of her employees was working the register, and she didn't seem in a hurry to get back. "I was worried when I saw the crêperie was closed. It's not permanent, is it?"

"No, I'll be reopening next week. With everything that happened, well, it didn't seem right to have it open right now."

Dora nodded, her cheerful expression sobering. "I heard one of your employees had a big blowup fight with you that resulted in him quitting. No one seems sure if he came back looking for revenge and you defended yourself or something else happened."

Theresa wrinkled her nose. "I fired him, I didn't have anything to do with—"

Dora raised a hand. "Hey, *I* know you didn't. You don't have to convince me. I'm just letting you know what people have been saying. I don't know what happened, but I know you didn't go off the deep end and kill someone. I may not have known you long, but I like to think I'm a better judge of character than that. Have the police made any progress in the case? The sooner you can clear your name, the better."

"Not that they've posted online." Theresa sighed. "How bad do you think it will be, when I reopen?"

Dora wiggled her hand back and forth, a gesture of uncertainty. "It could go either way. People like you, they like your food, but they also like drama and gossip, and an employer shooting her employee after a fight is a lot juicier than whatever really happened probably is. My advice is to figure out what you're going to say about it *before* people ask, and then hold firm to it. Don't change your story, and don't give out any more information than you have to. You've got another employee, right? Keep her front and center. Show that you aren't some psycho who is terrible to the people who work for you."

"That is some very useful advice," Theresa said. "Thank you."

Dora smiled and patted her shoulder. "You're a good woman, Theresa. You've got a good thing going with that crêperie. You'll get through this. I'm sure of it."

Dora returned to working the register, and Theresa picked up her sandwich. She hadn't realized how hungry she was, and the first bite was bliss.

She and Liam ate in silence for a few minutes, their hunger keeping them from talking. When conversation came again, he didn't ask about the crêperie, for which she was grateful.

"There's a theatre a couple of towns over that's putting on a new play I've heard some good things about," he ventured. "I plan on going, and it would be nice to have some company. Would you be interested in coming along with me?"

She considered the question. Liam had asked her out on a date before, but he knew she wasn't ready to enter a relationship yet. He had offered to be friends, and she trusted him not to try to make more of it than she was comfortable with. And it had been a long time since she had seen a play. She smiled at him.

"I think that sounds wonderful. I'd love to go."

He smiled back, and she returned her attention to her food. *Would I be this excited about going to a play with Clare?* She wondered, feeling the flush in her cheeks. She knew the answer was no. She just hoped she wasn't getting in over her head.

CHAPTER SEVEN

The week passed slowly, and when her alarm went off at six Wednesday morning, she was almost glad. She was eager to get back to some semblance of normal life.

The sun was coming up by the time she got to the crêperie, and Wynne arrived to help her open a few minutes after she unlocked the doors.

She was a little worried about how the reopening would go over with her customers, but while they weren't as busy as normal, no one did anything worse than give her a few sidelong looks as they accepted their food. She figured the people who most strongly believed she had something to do with Josh's death were simply avoiding the place.

It was a shame, but it was probably the best solution for all involved. She hoped they would change their minds when Josh's real killer was caught, but she wasn't holding her breath that it would happen anytime soon.

The dip in business was bad for her bank account, but on the upside, when the food truck came, she had enough time to help Wynne unload it and begin stocking the fresh produce. She was arranging the avocados from oldest to newest when Wynne leaned against the counter beside her.

"I know it's only been a week, but do you think you will hire someone new soon? Not that I'm complaining about the hours, but I think this place needs more than two people long term."

"I will," Theresa said. She'd already thought about it and knew it wasn't something she could put off forever. "I think I'll post the ad Monday. I'm a little worried we won't get any applicants if what happened is still too fresh on everyone's mind."

"I can ask around, see if anyone I know is interested in a job."

"That would be great, Wynne. They'll get the same starting pay and hours as you. Just have them drop off a resume, no application needed if it's someone you know."

"Do you think you'd ever hire more than one

other person?" Wynne asked, reaching over to help her with the avocados.

Theresa nodded. "I plan to, eventually. But there are a lot of hidden costs to having an employee. Beyond what I pay for your salary, I also have to pay more in taxes, including things like unemployment insurance. It's expensive to have people working for me, even when they're not actively on the clock. A lot of new restaurants fail—I think something like only twenty percent make it past the first five years. I don't want to spread myself too thin and end up having to shut my doors a couple years from now. But, I don't want to lose you either. Have you been content with the amount of work you were getting, before I let Josh go?"

"It was okay," Wynne said. "The hours themselves aren't bad, but it would be difficult to take time off. There's no one to cover for one of us if we get sick or need a vacation."

That was a good point. She had experienced the issue herself when she fired Josh and then had to go in on her day off. While she could run the crêperie on her own—and had, for months—she knew it was far from ideal, and she wasn't about to ask her employees to do the same. There really needed to be at least two people on the clock each day. Having two people working while one was off worked well, until someone wanted some time off, or got the flu, or had a family emergency.

"I don't think I can hire someone else right away, but I can look at the finances, and I can try to hire someone within the next month or two—in addition to the person we're hiring to replace Josh's position. Will that work for you?"

Wynne nodded. "Yeah, for sure. I think four employees is a good number for this place. And I want you to know—I *like* working here. Even if the hours get to be too much or something, I'll talk to you first. I won't just quit out of the blue."

Theresa smiled. "Thanks. That means a lot. I want this to be a good place to work. I've worked unpleasant jobs in the past and don't want to put anyone through that."

They continued working in peaceful quiet for a while. The order had included some twenty-pound bags of flour, and now that she was done with the fruit, she went out to the pallet and heaved a bag over her shoulder. Inside, she dropped it on the counter and as she did so, her elbow bumped Wynne's purse, sending it to the floor.

She stooped out of reflex to pick it up, then froze when she saw what had fallen out of it. Nestled among the earbuds, wallet, loose change, and other odds and ends, was a holstered pistol.

She stared at it, not sure what to do, until Wynne came over.

"Is everything all—" She broke off, and dropped to her knees to put the items back in her purse. When she looked up at Theresa, her eyes were wide. "I'm so sorry, I should've zipped my purse shut. I have a concealed carry license—I can legally carry the gun, but I still should've asked you before bringing it."

"Have you been bringing that to work this entire time?" Theresa asked, feeling uncertain. She had an old shotgun Nick had gotten from his grandfather, and she'd been to the shooting range a few times. But she wasn't exactly comfortable around guns, especially not in public like this.

Wynne shook her head. She carefully zipped her purse shut and put it back on the counter. "This is the first time. I got my concealed carry license a while ago but haven't used it much. But after what happened to Josh…"

She trailed off but didn't need to elaborate. Theresa understood, even if she wasn't sure how she felt about the situation.

She wished Wynne had asked her about it, and she wasn't comfortable with the gun just sitting in a purse on the counter. At the same time, how could she blame the younger woman for wanting to defend herself after what happened to Josh? She thought about asking her to keep it in the car, but that didn't seem ideal either. What if someone broke in and stole it?

"How about this?" she suggested after a few seconds. "I'll get a padlock for the cabinet we keep our jackets in, and you keep your purse locked in there while you're here. I know it will be a pain to have to undo the padlock every time one of us wants something out of the cabinet, but I'm not comfortable with it just sitting out."

"I think that's a good idea," Wynne said. "I'm sorry. I should have been more careful."

She should have, but she already seemed to feel bad enough, and Theresa wasn't going to make an issue of it. As long as it didn't happen again, it would be all right.

She walked over to the cabinet to examine it, trying to figure out what she would need to buy at the hardware store to fix a lock to it. She opened the door to judge how thick it was and spotted the hoodie and hat Josh had left behind still hanging inside it.

His belongings were still here, along with his check. She could mail it, but he only lived a few blocks away, and it seemed like a waste of time and money to go to the post office when she could just drop it off. Adrian could get the items back to his parents from there. It wouldn't take her long. She could go this afternoon and still be back to her apartment in time to start getting ready for her dinner with Clare and Clare's mystery man.

CHAPTER EIGHT

Wynne seemed embarrassed for the rest of the day, even though Theresa didn't bring up the gun again. It wasn't the worst day she'd ever had at the crêperie, but everyone seemed to be walking on eggshells—her employee, her customers, and even herself.

There was tension and uncertainty hanging over everything she did, and she hated it. She wished she could go back in time and keep Josh from being in the wrong place at the wrong time or go even further back and just prevent herself from hiring him at all.

Wynne seemed jumpy on top of being embarrassed, and that made Theresa feel even worse. She hadn't thought about how being here would affect the other woman. Not only was she being forced to deal with all of the memories of Josh and whatever she felt about the death of a man she hadn't even liked, but with his killer still out there, she might be in danger too.

The worry that his killer might be lurking nearby began to make Theresa nervous too. She started looking at her customers as they came in and wondering if one of them had been involved in the shooting. It seemed possible, or even likely, that his killer might return to the crêperie. Wasn't that something that happened on crime shows? Did killers really return to the scene of the crime?

When three o'clock finally came around, it was a relief to close. Theresa told herself things would get better with time, but she wished she knew how much time it would take. When would her life get back to normal? *Could* it get back to normal after something like this happened?

After closing, she grabbed Josh's hoodie and hat out of the cabinet and put them on the passenger seat of her car. She'd taken the chance to pull his file up on the computer and took a picture of his address. While she knew he lived close by, she had never actually been to the building before. It would be a while yet before she knew all of Crooked Bay like the back of her hand, no matter how small it was.

She typed the address in her GPS and pulled away from the curb, following the directions the program relayed to her in its robotic voice. It wasn't until she parked in front of the old, dated apartment building and reached for the hat and hoodie that she realized she had forgotten the most important item—Josh's check.

She hesitated and considered going back, but she was supposed to meet Clare and her mystery man at the restaurant at six, and it would take her half an hour to get there from her apartment. It was just past three thirty now—if she got home at four, that would leave her only an hour and a half to get ready to go. It *sounded* like a lot of time, but she knew just how quickly that time could vanish into nothing, and she didn't want to be late. She could drop off the check another day—or maybe Adrian would be willing to stop in during the day tomorrow to pick it up.

She grabbed the hoodie and the hat and walked up to the apartment building's entrance. Much like her own building, this one didn't have a buzzer or a lock. Anyone could let themselves in. She pulled the door open, double-checked the address on her phone, then took the stairs up to the second floor. Apartment 2B. She felt a surge of grief as it struck her that Josh would never see this door again, never come home again.

She took a deep breath and tried to clear the emotions away before she knocked on the door. She heard the creaking of old floorboards a second before the door opened as far as the chain would allow. Adrian looked out, his expression of bored curiosity turning to confusion when he saw her.

"Um—you're Josh's boss, aren't you?"

She nodded and gestured at the sweatshirt and hat she had in her arms. "He left some things at the crêperie, and I didn't know what to do with them. I thought I'd stop by to drop them off."

The door shut only to be reopened a second later after Adrian slid the chain off the latch. Theresa got a look at the apartment behind him. It was somehow both sparse and messy, and reminded her a little of Jace's college apartment before he got used to living on his own and realized no one would be picking up after him. It was a reminder of just how young Josh was. He hadn't made it past his early twenties. It was old enough that some people his age were starting families, but young enough that they were still practically kids themselves in her eyes.

Adrian took the sweatshirt and hat from her with a muttered thanks, but before he could shut the door, someone else approached across the creaky floor. Tabitha came into view, her eyes red rimmed. She seemed surprised to see Theresa there, and Theresa was just as surprised to see her.

"What's going on?" she asked, her voice rough from crying. She looked down at the hoodie in Adrian's hands and gasped. Adrian handed it over to her.

"She was just dropping off some of Josh's things.

"Hi, Tabitha," Theresa said. "How are you doing?"

Tabitha gave a halfhearted shrug, hugging the sweatshirt to her chest. "I'm all right, I guess." She didn't sound all right, but Theresa didn't press her. Adrian looked between them, frowning.

"Do you two know each other?"

Tabitha shook her head. "Not really, but I talked to her about what happened to Josh. She seems nice."

"Do you live here too?" Theresa asked, curious. She'd known Josh had one roommate, Adrian, but hadn't been aware Tabitha was also living with them. It wasn't any of her business, but she could only imagine how hard it must be if both of them were stuck renting an apartment together when Josh, the one who had linked them, was gone.

"Nah," Adrian said. "Just reminiscing, I guess. I still can't believe he's gone."

"Yeah," Tabitha said. "And being around some of his old things helps." She clung to his sweatshirt. "Thanks for bringing this over."

"Of course." She hesitated, looking between them. They were both upset, that much was clear. Adrian watched Tabitha with concern, and after a second, put the hat on his own head. She looked up, gave him a sad smile, then returned to gazing at the sweatshirt. Theresa wished she could do something to help them, but she couldn't. She knew no one could take this grief from them.

"I'll get out of your hair now." She didn't know what else to say—*Have a nice evening* was all wrong, and *I hope you feel better* felt too light. Instead, she just stepped back, and Adrian shut the door. Her heart heavy, she made her way back downstairs.

She might not have left things on good terms with Josh, but this visit had reminded her he was much more than just a lackluster employee. His death touched many lives, and none of them would ever be the same again.

Once she was outside of the apartment building, she stopped and looked back up. Tabitha stared down at her from the upper window for a long moment before the blinds pulled shut. Had one of them had something to do with Josh's death? Statistically, it might be likely, but it was hard to imagine it.

Shaking her head, she walked back to her car. His murderer would slip up at some point. The police would catch him—or her—and then people could start healing from this horrible, horrible mess.

CHAPTER NINE

Theresa arrived to dinner just in the nick of time. It was a little sushi restaurant a few towns away from Crooked Bay, and the mouthwatering scent when she stepped through the doors reminded her how long it had been since she'd eaten something more exotic than a crêpe. She loved Crooked Bay, but it didn't have the greatest variety of restaurants.

She paused just inside the door and looked around the dining area. It only took a second to spot Clare. Her cousin had already seen her and was waving at her. Theresa waved back and headed over. She was sitting alone at a small table against the back wall, and Theresa raised an eyebrow at the three empty seats as she approached.

"It's good to see you, but where's the mystery man?"

Clare made a face. "I know you're disappointed, but he had a family emergency at the last minute and couldn't make it."

Theresa gave her a skeptical look as she sat down. It sounded like a made-up excuse, and at this point, she wasn't sure if this man actually existed or not. She liked to think her cousin hadn't gone completely off the deep end, but they had been seriously dating for over a month, and she still hadn't even seen a picture of the guy.

"Don't look at me like that," Clare said. "He's real, he's just got a lot going on. You'll meet him soon."

"I hope so." She set her purse down on the chair next to her. The server approached to take their drink orders and give them menus. "Have you eaten here before?"

Clare nodded. "It's a favorite of ours. All of the dishes I've tried so far have been good. I don't remember if you like sushi or not, but they have plenty of other options if you don't. The udon noodles are great, but if you *do* like sushi, their specialty rolls are to die for."

Theresa rarely craved sushi, but when she did

have it, she liked it. It had been a long time since she'd had the occasion to try any—years, she realized. She considered the menu and marked off the two rolls she wanted to try—one a deep-fried roll with softshell crab and eel, and the other a salmon and cream cheese roll topped with mango sauce.

After checking her selection with the dry-erase marker the server had dropped off along with the laminated menus, she put the menu down and looked at Clare, who had already made her own choices. It was good to see her cousin, even if she wasn't going to meet her cousin's date.

"So, this mystery man, what does he do for a living?"

"It's complicated," Clare said. "Look, just wait until you meet him, okay? I get the feeling you wouldn't believe me even if I told you."

Theresa sighed but did her best to push her curiosity aside for now. "Then what should we talk about?"

"Have the police figured out who killed your employee yet?" Clare asked.

Theresa waited until the waiter came back to take their menus and give them their drinks before she replied. "No, and there haven't been any updates online either. That doesn't mean they're not working behind the scenes, of course, but it's discouraging. I know police work is a lot slower in real life than it is in the movies, but I want results. I'm not comfortable working at the crêperie knowing one of our customers might have killed Josh, and neither is Wynne."

"Do you think you might not be safe at work?" Clare asked with a frown.

Theresa shifted. "I really don't know. I don't know *why* Josh was murdered. I don't know if it had something to do with the crêperie, or if it had something to do with his personal life, or if it was completely random. But…" She hesitated. "Wynne doesn't feel safe. I found out today that she brought a gun to work. It makes me uncomfortable, but at the same time I understand it. If I was more comfortable with guns and could legally carry one, I might do the same thing. I hate that I'm putting her in a position where she feels so uncomfortable. And I learned Josh was making her uncomfortable when they worked together, too. I feel guilty about that on top of everything else."

Clare frowned. "So your employee—Wynne, right?—had issues with Josh, and she owns a gun. And whoever killed Josh shot him. Doesn't that seem kind of suspicious to you?"

Theresa's stomach clenched. The connection

wasn't one she'd made on her own yet. She *liked* Wynne. They got along well, and the other woman seemed pleasant and responsible. She considered it for a moment, but… "No, she left a few minutes before he got there that afternoon. It couldn't have been her."

"Are you sure? I mean, if she wasn't in your line of sight, you don't really know where she was, do you?"

Theresa pursed her lips, thinking. Clare had a point. She didn't actually know if Wynne had left. For all she knew, she had been sitting in her car in the back parking lot until Josh arrived. The more she thought about it, the more sense it made. What if she had gotten into a confrontation with Josh? If she had her gun with her and the confrontation escalated, maybe she had shot him in self-defense—or what she thought was self-defense.

She shook her head, trying to think of someone else, anyone else it could be. "There are other suspects," she said, though of course it wasn't really Clare she had to convince. "There was this guy, Bill Mason, a regular. He and Josh had a disagreement the day before. He's not the most pleasant person to be around, and he seems like the type to hold grudges.

It's possible he ran into Josh outside the crêperie and decided to escalate things."

Clare gave a skeptical frown. "Bill Mason? I know him. His wife was a client of mine. She passed away a few years back. He contacted me a while after she passed and asked if I offered sessions as a medium. That's one of the things I won't do—it feels too much like taking advantage of my clients. I told him as much and haven't heard from him since, but from what I know, he's not a bad guy. He's just had a really bad few years and is missing his wife. I'm not saying he didn't do it, but he doesn't exactly strike me as the type to shoot someone over a tiff at a restaurant."

She hadn't known any of that. Theresa's heart went out to Bill. She knew just what he was going through, and she understood some of his behavior better now. It was hard to think of anyone other than yourself when you were mired in the sort of grief he was experiencing.

She sighed, leaning back as the waiter approached with their food. She thanked him, unwrapped the chopsticks they had given her, and looked at her plate. The food looked and smelled delicious, but she had a weight on her chest that she hadn't before. It *couldn't* be Wynne. She didn't believe it was, not really, but Clare's words had stuck with her.

Trying to focus on her meal, she picked up a piece of sushi with her chopsticks and popped it into her mouth. It was good, but she would enjoy it a lot more if her mind wasn't on murder.

CHAPTER TEN

It was dark by the time Theresa left the restaurant with Clare. She followed her cousin toward Crooked Bay, her stomach full but her mind hungry for answers. She knew Clare had been right to point it out, but a part of her resented her cousin for planting the seed of doubt in her mind about Wynne. How was she going to feel comfortable working alongside her employee now?

But really, what did she know about the younger woman? Wynne had only worked for her for a few weeks, and Theresa hadn't even run a background check on her, though she had gotten the information needed to do so and Wynne had signed a consent form for it. It had seemed like an unnecessary expense at the time—how much of a criminal could a twenty-something-year-old woman be?—but now she regretted it.

Maybe she could still do it. There were websites that offered instant background checks, weren't there? It wouldn't tell her whether or not Wynne had killed Josh, but at least it might tell her if she had a reason to be worried.

She turned the thought over in her mind as she followed her cousin toward town. It didn't feel quite right, going behind Wynne's back to do a background check on her, but she *had* given her consent back when she first applied for the job. This was the same background check Theresa should have done in the first place just … delayed. Despite her rationalization, she was still uncomfortable with it, but the thought of working with the person who had killed Josh made her even more uncomfortable.

When Clare turned toward her own home, in the opposite direction from where Theresa was going, Theresa gave a quiet honk goodbye, and continued to her apartment. It felt good to get home. She had been gone most of the day, having only stopped in briefly to change before she left again for dinner.

Inside, she took a moment to change into more comfortable clothes and make herself a cup of tea before she sat down at the coffee table with her laptop. She searched for online background checks and looked through the websites that came up until she found one that looked somewhat trustworthy. She got up to get her credit card and a copy of the information Wynne had given her when Theresa first hired her, then sat back down in front of her laptop.

She hesitated a second longer but decided this was something she should have done anyway. Going forward, she would do all of the background checks for new employees right away instead of putting them off because she didn't think they were necessary.

She typed in the information and paid for the check, then waited for the results, drumming her fingers on top of the coffee table. It didn't take long for the information to load, and when it did, the results were ... lackluster. Nothing popped out. Wynne didn't have a single red flag. Her record reflected the same person she seemed to be in real life —a normal, responsible young woman with no dark past to hide.

She moved the cursor to exit out of the window, but hesitated. What about Josh? She hadn't done a background check on him, either. He had signed all the same consent forms Wynne had, and while it wouldn't exactly help if she learned he had a dark past now, it might help her figure out who had shot him.

She got up again to get his file and typed in his information. When the results popped up, one of the sections was highlighted in red. She clicked on it and saw that there had been an aggravated assault charge against him a few years ago, shortly after he got out of high school. There wasn't much information available, but the gist of it seemed to be that he had gotten into a fight, been charged, and had been sentenced to do community service for a while.

She frowned, trying to figure out what it meant or if it meant anything at all. She supposed it told her Josh had an issue with violence in the past. Maybe the shooting had been in self-defense after all, or maybe it was completely unrelated to his charges.

With a sigh, she saved the results and then shut her laptop. Her tea was lukewarm by now, and she drank it in a few gulps. Maybe she needed more if she wanted the chamomile to do its job. She didn't exactly feel relaxed.

Someone knocked on the door. She jolted, feeling jumpy, then set the teacup down on the table and got up. When she looked out the peephole, she felt some of the tension leave her. It was just her next-door neighbor, Grace.

Theresa unlocked the door and pulled it open, only to be immediately greeted by Grace's large, gray dog, Atticus. He jumped forward, his tail whipping against Grace's legs as he leaned into her legs, looking for attention. She bent over to scratch behind his ears and pat his sides before straightening up to look at her neighbor. Grace smiled at her.

"I know it's dark out, but do you want to go for a walk? We could just go up and down the beach. Atticus is going stir crazy tonight. He always barks more when he gets like this, so I want him to get some of this energy out."

"Sure. Give me a second to grab my shoes and my keys."

She left the door open as she found her tennis shoes and snagged her keys, then locked the door behind her before following Grace and Atticus out of the apartment building. She had started taking walks with the two of them a few weeks ago, after getting to know Grace better during the chaos that ensued when one of the other residents in their building passed away.

Atticus was a big, energetic dog and didn't do well being cooped up. The first time Theresa joined them on a walk, she had just happened to run into them when they were going down to the beach. Grace had invited her along, and Theresa had enjoyed it, both getting some exercise with a companion and watching the dog lope joyfully along the shore. She missed having a dog of her own. Their family dog had passed a couple years before Nick was diagnosed, and they had wanted to travel before committing to another pet. Now she knew she worked too many hours for her to be able to give one the attention it deserved. Atticus was quickly becoming her substitute for a dog of her own.

It was dark, but Theresa had her phone as a flashlight, and Grace had a headlamp. She bent down and fiddled with her dog's collar, and it started to glow a bright, neon green. He pulled at the end of his leash as they stepped into the parking lot, but Grace paused and waited for the leash to go slack before they continued on.

They crossed the road, followed the narrow path down to the beach, then started walking along the shore. Once Grace saw it was empty, she unclipped the leash and Atticus took off like a shot, his glowing collar moving like a shooting star through the dark.

"How are you doing?" Grace asked. "I've been meaning to check in on you, but we keep missing each other."

"I'm still trying to get back to normal after what

happened to my employee," Theresa said. "I really wish the police could hurry up and catch his killer so all of this can just be over."

"Do you have any theories about who might have done it?"

Theresa shared Clare's thought of Wynne possibly shooting him during an argument and mentioned the conflict between him and Bill Mason. Grace considered her responses, then asked, "What about family or friends? Did he have a girlfriend? It's usually people the victims know, isn't it?"

"He had a girlfriend, but she wasn't even in town at the time of his death, so it couldn't have been her."

"I wonder how good her alibi was," Grace mused. "Maybe I watch too many true crime shows, but I feel like the killer usually ends up being the significant other."

While Tabitha must have given the police an alibi, Theresa realized all she had to go on was the other woman's word. What if Tabitha *had* been lying to her? Josh had seemed certain she was going to give him a ride in. Wouldn't he know if she was out of town?

She frowned, wishing she knew exactly what had transpired in the interview room with Tabitha and the detective who had questioned her, but it was a futile wish. The police were keeping everything about this case quiet.

"I really don't envy the detectives their jobs," Grace said, interrupting her thoughts. She watched as Atticus ran back and forth ahead of them. "I don't know how they can make progress on cases without any obvious suspects. Unless I caught the suspect red-handed at the scene of the crime, I'd be completely stumped. But then, I'm the sort of person who never guesses the right suspect when I'm reading murder mysteries, so maybe I'm just extra bad at putting the clues together."

"I'm glad I'm not a police detective," Theresa said. "I like piecing together mysteries, but I'd never want to have so much pressure on me. It must be hard for them, whenever a dangerous criminal slips through their fingers."

Still, a part of her wished she had the power to *do* something. She felt like she could almost see what had happened but was missing the last few pieces of the puzzle.

CHAPTER ELEVEN

She tried not to let her discomfort around Wynne show when they opened the restaurant together the next morning. When she spotted the other woman put her purse in the cabinet, she realized that between dropping Josh's items off at his apartment and meeting Clare for dinner, she had completely forgotten to go to the hardware store and pick up what she needed to attach a padlock to it.

They still weren't as busy as usual, so that afternoon, after the worst of the lunch rush was over, she sent Wynne off to the hardware store to pick up the supplies. It was strange, being in the crêperie alone again. Or rather, it was strange how quickly she'd gotten used to having her employees there to help her. In between customers, she started drafting an ad to post for a new hire. Wynne was right; the two of them really weren't enough to run this place on their own. She would post it first thing Monday morning, and hopefully, she'd have a new employee by the end of the week.

When Wynne returned from the hardware store, Theresa thanked her and brought the bag into the back. Before she could start installing the lock, she heard the door chime twice and stepped back into the dining area to see if Wynne needed help. She did; they were getting a rush right before close.

The additional business made time fly by, and before she knew it, it was time to lock the door and turn the open sign over so it read *Closed* to the outside world. With that done, she turned to Wynne.

"You can head out, if you'd like. I'll finish up here."

"Are you sure? We still have to clean."

"Don't worry about it," Theresa said. "I don't have anything else to do this afternoon. I'm happy to finish up here on my own."

She gave the other woman a reassuring smile, but the truth was she just wasn't completely comfortable around Wynne after her discussion with Clare. She hoped something would change soon, but for now, she would much rather finish the closing routine alone, even if it took her a little longer than it would otherwise.

Once Wynne left, Theresa locked the doors and finished cleaning the dining area before returning to the kitchen to work on the lock. She had bought some used power tools back when she was first setting up the crêperie and had kept them there since she wasn't about to start any big improvement projects at her apartment. Now, she got out her drill and a box of screws and got to work.

When she was done, she left a sticky note with the combination lock's code next to the schedule. She would take it down eventually, but for now, she didn't want to have to look the code up every time someone needed to get into the cabinet. She was proud of herself. It hadn't been a big project, but it wasn't the sort of thing she would have done on her own back when Nicolas was still around. It was satisfying to work with her hands like this, even if it was just a small thing.

She stepped forward and unlocked the cabinet, making sure the lock worked. Her eyes caught on a piece of paper sitting on the top shelf. It was a check —Josh's check. She had forgotten it when she brought his sweatshirt and hat to the apartment, and then it slipped her mind with everything else she had done yesterday.

She decided to stop by the apartment again before she went home. If Adrian wasn't there, maybe she could slip it into the mailbox. She just wanted to be done with this. His death was going to haunt her for long enough as it was. She didn't need this check haunting her too.

She slipped the check into her purse, put her tools away, and left for the day. She had finally started parking behind the building again, and her steps faltered when she walked out into the parking lot. It was sunny now, and there was a truck parked over the place Josh had died, but that rainy afternoon was burned into her memory. She didn't think it would ever fade.

She didn't need to type his address in this time; the apartment was close and easy to find. She parked in front of the building, double-checked that the check was in her purse, and got out of her car. As she approached the building, the front door opened, and Tabitha came out, carrying a cardboard box in her arms. She had fresh tears on her face, and Theresa's steps faltered. The younger woman looked at her and came to a stop.

"What are you doing here? Did he leave something else at work?"

"I'm bringing Josh's last check. I need to get it to his parents, or whoever is in charge of his estate. Are *you* okay?"

"I left some of my things here, and Adrian said I could take a few of Josh's items too. I can't keep coming back here. It's too hard. I'm just going to take all my stuff and go."

"Do you need help?"

Tabitha hesitated, then nodded. "There are a couple more boxes upstairs. If you want to come up and drop the check off, we could both carry one down, and I wouldn't have to make another trip."

Theresa agreed, so she waited while Tabitha dropped the box off in her car, then followed the other woman up the stairs. Tabitha reached the landing first and pushed the door to Adrian and Josh's shared apartment open. Theresa climbed the last of the stairs and turned towards the apartment in time to see Adrian grab Tabitha's wrist as she tried to walk by him.

"Why won't you just talk to me? I—" He broke off, looking over her shoulder at Theresa, and released her wrist. Theresa frowned, feeling a prickle of unease. Tabitha turned back to her, rubbing her wrist.

"Come on in," she said. "You can drop the check off, and I'll show you the boxes."

Uncomfortable, and uncertain if this was the right choice, Theresa stepped into the apartment. Tabitha reached over and pushed the door shut. It closed with a click behind Theresa's back.

CHAPTER TWELVE

"What is she doing here?" Adrian asked, looking at Tabitha and then at Theresa, his brows furrowed.

Theresa cleared her throat and reached into her purse. "I have Josh's last paycheck. Legally, I can't just keep it. Do you know how to contact his parents? If so, can I just leave it with you?"

Adrian looked down at the check in her hand and blinked. "Sure. Let me just go grab my phone. I'll shoot them a text." He looked over at Tabitha. "Please, just stay, and we can talk this out."

He didn't wait for a response before turning and heading into the other room. Tabitha looked after him uncertainly, then moved over to the boxes on the dining table and started folding their tops shut.

Theresa frowned, watching her. It had been a long

time since she'd been young, and maybe things had changed, but the degree of closeness between Tabitha and Adrian didn't seem normal. When she was their age, she couldn't imagine any of her boyfriends being so close to her roommate that they spent time hanging out together alone, but she remembered a few times when Adrian and Tabitha had come into the crêperie together. Something in the way Adrian had looked at her just now felt deeper than friendship to her.

"Tabitha," she started, hesitant as she tried to figure out what to say. "Is everything all right here?" That was the most important thing. She remembered how Adrian had grabbed the other woman. She didn't like it.

"It's fine," Tabitha said. "It just—we've been going through a lot. Ever since Josh…" She trailed off and rubbed her eyes. "And I like Adrian, I do, but he just wants too much. It's only been a week. I'm not even close to ready to think about a relationship."

"Adrian's interested in starting a relationship?" Theresa asked. Talk about moving fast. She wouldn't be comfortable with it either, in Tabitha's shoes.

"I know it sounds bad, but he's always had a thing for me, and I think Josh's death made him realize how fleeting life is. I *do* like him; it's just too soon."

Was this the missing piece? "The day Josh died,"

she said, keeping her voice quiet as she moved closer, "was Adrian the one who gave him a ride to the crêperie?"

Theresa blinked, looking uncertain. "Maybe. He works nights, so he's here all day almost every day. But if he was asleep, Josh wouldn't have woken him up to ask."

It began to make sense. Of a sort. Adrian had been hiding feelings for Tabitha for who knew how long, and it must have driven him crazy to see her spending time with his roommate every day. Her gut told her she was on the right track.

"Tabitha, I think you might be in danger here. I'll help you bring the last of your stuff down, then we should go. I'll leave the check on the table and—"

She heard a door close and fell silent as Adrian came out of the other room with his cell phone. "All right, I called them, but they didn't answer. If you want to just leave the check here, I'll mail it to them, I guess. I've got a bunch of his stuff I need to send to them anyway, so I'll just do it all at once."

"Thanks, Adrian," she said, dropping the check on the dining table next to Tabitha's boxes. "Can I help you bring a box down, Tabitha?" she asked, looking into the other woman's eyes pointedly. The other woman hesitated.

"Look, I know you're worried, but I want to talk to Adrian before I go."

"Are you sure?" Theresa's heart ached at the thought of leaving the other woman here alone. Whatever was going on, Tabitha was vulnerable, and Adrian didn't seem to respect her current state.

Tabitha wavered, unsure. "Hey, what's this about?" Adrian asked. He stepped between the two of them. "You're going to stay and talk to me, right? I don't want to leave things like this."

She gave him an uncomfortable look. "I'm going to bring these boxes down with Theresa while she's here. She offered to help and—"

"She doesn't have to help you. I'll bring them down for you when we're done talking."

"Adrian, I really just want to get this done now—"

"There's no rush," he said. "Why are you in a hurry to go?"

"I just don't want to put it off," she said, reaching for a box. He grabbed her wrist, and she jerked her hand away from him, shooting him a dark look. He backed up, raising his hands as he retreated to the couch. "Sorry, sorry. You'll come back up, right?"

Tabitha exchanged a glance with Theresa. "Sure. I just want to drop these off in my car first."

Theresa turned to grab a box, and Tabitha picked up her own. Behind her, she heard the sound of a wooden drawer sliding open, and out of the corner of her eye she saw Tabitha freeze. The cardboard box slipped out of her hands and fell to the floor with a thud.

Theresa dropped her own box back onto the table and turned around, her heart leaping into her throat when she saw Adrian standing by the coffee table. He had left the drawer open. Both his hands were occupied with the handgun, which he was pointing right at them.

"Just hear me out, Tabitha. If you go out that door, you'll never give me a chance to say what I want to say."

"Why—why do you have a gun?" Tabitha stammered.

"It's for your own good. I don't want you to leave until I get a chance to say my piece. I love you, don't you know that?"

"If you loved her, you wouldn't be pointing a gun at her," Theresa said, certain she was about to witness a second murder.

The gun turned toward her, and she wished she hadn't spoken. "It's for her own good," he repeated. "She's scared of what she's feeling. She needs to listen to what I have to say and accept her own feelings, that's all. No one else in the world cares for her like I do. You're just like everyone else. You want to tear us apart."

"Adrian!" Tabitha said. "Stop it. Put the gun down. Theresa was just trying to help."

"Trying to take you away from me isn't helping," he said. "It's not any of her business. I just want to talk to you."

"Why do you have a gun, Adrian?" Tabitha repeated, her voice catching. "I didn't know you had a gun." She faltered, then said, "Did you shoot Josh?"

"I was just protecting you," Adrian told her. He seemed earnest, frighteningly so. The fact that he didn't seem to realize how insane this was frightened Theresa. "He was going to ask you to move in with him. He told me about it in the car on the way to the crêperie when I drove him to pick up his things. He was saving his money to move out and was going to ask you to move in with him when he did. He was complaining because he couldn't afford to do it anymore after he got fired, and it would have to wait until he found another job. It was a blessing in disguise, of course. If he moved away, when would I get to see you, Tabitha? I couldn't let him take you away from me, even far off in the future. I told him you should both just live with me, but he thought that was ridiculous. I think he finally realized how I felt about you then. I wish it hadn't come to that. He was my friend. But I would do it again, Tabitha. I would do it for you."

The obsession in his eyes scared Theresa more than anger would have. He looked irrational, crazed.

"You ...you shot Josh?" Tabitha's voice came out in a whisper, barely audible.

Theresa shot a glance toward the younger woman. She looked on the verge of a breakdown, and she didn't blame her for it, but they had to hold it together. She didn't know what Adrian would do if Tabitha rejected him now.

"We belong together, Tabitha. I know you love me too. There's nothing keeping us apart now. You don't have to take your things away. Leave them here. Move in with me."

Tabitha jerked back as if he had struck her, and her expression filled with disgust. Theresa knew that whatever she was about to say wouldn't be good and opened her mouth to cut the other woman off when a jingling ringtone cut through the quiet in the apartment. Adrian glanced down at the coffee table where his cell phone was. There was a flicker in his expression. Was it regret? Sadness? "It's Josh's parents. They're calling about the check, probably."

He was distracted, but only for a moment. Theresa looked over at Tabitha, but the other woman was frozen. Adrian was reaching down to mute the call, the gun wavering and his attention off them, and she knew she only had a second. The apartment was small. She could make it to him in just a few steps.

She made her decision and rushed forward before she had time to regret it. Adrian looked up at the last second, but it was too late. She caught his wrist with her hand and pushed it up. His finger was on the trigger and the gun went off, but the bullet buried itself harmlessly in the ceiling. She was glad they were on the upper floor, so they didn't have to worry about someone above them being hurt.

Tabitha screamed.

"Run, Tabitha," Theresa said. "Get help!"

Out of the corner of her eye, she saw the other woman flee through the front door. She felt relieved, but it was a temporary flicker in the face of the danger she was in. Adrian swore at her and tried to yank the gun away, but she stepped on his insole, remembering some half-forgotten self-defense instructions. He yelped and stumbled back, and she used both her wrists to keep his hand with the gun in it pointing up.

The gun went off again, and he swore, his other hand reaching for her face or her throat. She leaned back as far she could while keeping a grip on his wrist. He started trying to pry her fingers off of him. The gun went off a third time.

Faintly, through the ringing in her ears, she heard Tabitha yell, "Hurry!"

The other woman ran in through the open apartment door, followed by a bulky man. He gave a shout when he saw the struggle in the living room and rushed over to wrap an arm around Adrian's throat from behind. Adrian struggled for a moment but finally dropped the gun. Theresa released his wrist, bent to pick up the gun, and backed away. She turned to look at Tabitha, who was staring, wide eyed, as if a part of her still couldn't believe it.

"I went to get Mike," she said. Theresa assumed that was the man who had subdued Adrian. "He lives downstairs and is always home. Do you have a phone? We need the police."

Theresa grabbed Adrian's phone, which was the closest at hand, and dialed 911, her hands shaking. Adrian was trying to pull Mike's arm off of him, but it was futile.

Tabitha watched, horrified, as one of the people she trusted most swore and kicked and tried to get free just so he could hurt her. Theresa felt a pang as the dispatcher answered. She hoped Tabitha wouldn't blame herself for what had happened. Even though Adrian *had* shot Josh over her, it wasn't her fault. It was Adrian, his obsession, and his delusion. She hoped Adrian came to realize just how much he lost when he decided murder was the way to a girl's heart.

EPILOGUE

"One s'more crêpe to share."

Theresa's newest employee set the plate down between her and Clare, along with two forks. She had hired him the week before, and so far had no regrets.

He was a newcomer to Crooked Bay, just like her, and was a single father. She didn't know all the details, just that he had moved to town so his parents could help him raise his young daughter. The hours were just about perfect for him—his daughter was starting school this fall, and he would be able to come in half an hour after open, after he dropped her off, and leave half an hour before close to pick her up. On the days he worked, the other person on the schedule would have to open and close alone, but she would boost their pay for that extra hour to make it worth it.

She had let Wynne sit in on the interviews, and Kian was the one they had both liked the most. He might have some constraints with his schedule, but he had a lot of restaurant experience, which more than made up for it. He had worked as a waiter in the past and had been a line cook at a Chinese food restaurant before this. He also seemed likable and easy to get along with—a necessity for anyone she was going to spend a large portion of the day with.

"Thanks, Kian," she said. "You have no idea how weird it feels to have someone else serving me food in my own restaurant. You're doing a great job."

He grinned, then left them to their meal so he could help another customer. She was taking a break —which was such a nice concept—but she would get up to help him if he needed it. Already she was beginning to wonder how she had managed to run the crêperie on her own for so long.

"Okay, it looks like we can do next Saturday. Would that work?" Clare asked.

Theresa pulled her attention back to the conversation she and her cousin were having. "Saturday evening?"

Clare nodded. "I'm not sure of the exact time yet, but it will definitely be after the crêperie is closed."

"Sure, that's fine with me. Am I really going to meet the guy this time, Clare?"

"Yes. What happened last time was just a fluke."

Theresa wasn't so sure about that but didn't say anything. She reached for a fork and took a bite of her crêpe, savoring the sweet dessert. Clare took her own bite from the opposite side and gave a contented hum.

Theresa's phone buzzed, so she pulled it out of her pocket and glanced at the screen. It was a text message from Liam, and she felt a smile come unbidden to her face as she unlocked the screen and started typing a reply. She had tomorrow off and had been talking about coming into the bookstore to help him sort through a new delivery of used books. They had seen a play together this past weekend, and while they had both been very clear that it wasn't a date, she had left with the feeling that maybe it was. And maybe that was okay.

Sorting through used books with him wasn't exactly a date either, but she still felt inordinately eager as she typed out her response.

"Theresa. *Theresa.*"

She looked up to see Clare gazing at her with an eyebrow quirked. "Did you hear anything I just said?"

"Ah..." She glanced down at the food. "The crêpe is good?"

Clare snorted, but she looked more amused than annoyed. "You're staring at your phone like when Jace was a teenager and he had his first girlfriend. Is there anything you'd like to tell me?"

Theresa sent the message and put her phone back into her pocket. "I've got no idea what you're talking about," she said lightly. She stabbed another bite of the crêpe. "And this crêpe *is* good. I need to come up with a new special soon, though. The eggs Benedict crêpe went over well, but that hollandaise sauce is a pain to make throughout the day. Start brainstorming ideas with me. I need something easy, tasty, and something everyone loves, and it needs to make sense in crêpe form."

Clare sighed. "You are obviously changing the subject, but I'll let it go since you've been so patient about my 'mystery man,' as you call him. So, crêpes..."

They brainstormed ideas as they ate, Kian keeping the crêperie running smoothly around them while they chatted. It felt nice. Peaceful. It had been just months since she left her old life behind, and already it seemed like a long-ago memory.

It was bittersweet, but Theresa was happier now. That was what Nicolas would have wanted for her, and just as importantly, it was what she wanted for herself. She would always have her memories, and she was beginning to realize that embracing a new future didn't mean losing what she cherished about the past.

Printed in Great Britain
by Amazon